W9-AAW-130

CHLOE *by* DESIGN

ALL OR *Nothing*

BY MARGARET GUREVICH

ILLUSTRATIONS BY BROOKE HAGEL

STONE ARCH BOOKS
a capstone imprint

Chloe by Design is published by Stone Arch Books
A Capstone Imprint
1710 Roe Crest Drive
North Mankato, MN 56003
www.mycapstone.com

Text and illustrations © 2016 Stone Arch Books

All rights reserved. No part of this publication may be reproduced in whole
or in part, or stored in a retrieval system, or transmitted in any form or by
any means, electronic, mechanical, photocopying, recording, or otherwise,
without written permission of the publisher.

Library of Congress Cataloging-in-Publication Data

Names: Gurevich, Margaret, author. | Hagel, Brooke, illustrator. |
Gurevich, Margaret. Chloe by design. Title: All or nothing / by Margaret
Gurevich ; illustrations by Brooke Hagel.
Description: North Mankato, Minnesota : Stone Arch Books, a Capstone
imprint, [2016] | Series: Chloe by design | Summary: Chloe and Nina
have always been rivals, but now, as they create fashion portfolios for their
college applications, they have come to respect and like each other, and
working together is proving beneficial — but Chloe's best friend Alex is
jealous of the amount of time the two are spending together.
Identifiers: LCCN 2016008003 | ISBN 9781496532633 (hardcover) | ISBN
9781496532671 (ebook pdf)
Subjects: LCSH: Fashion design--Juvenile fiction. | High school
seniors--Juvenile fiction. | College applications--Juvenile fiction. | Best
friends--Juvenile fiction. | Friendship--Juvenile fiction. | Santa Cruz
(Calif.)--Juvenile fiction. | CYAC: Fashion design--Fiction. | High
schools--Fiction. | Schools--Fiction. | College applications--Fiction. | Best
friends--Fiction. | Friendship--Fiction. | Santa Cruz (Calif.)--Fiction.
Classification: LCC PZ7.G98146 Al 2016 | DDC 813.6--dc23
LC record available at http://lccn.loc.gov/2016008003

Designer: Alison Thiele
Editor: Alison Deering

Artistic Elements: Shutterstock

Printed in Canada.
009628F16

Measure twice, cut once
or you won't make the cut.

Dear Diary,

I think I'm finally getting the hang of this college application thing. Or, at least, I'm not panicking as much as before. There are still a lot of portfolio requirements to complete, but I'm actually starting to feel like I'll get them all done. Believe it or not, I have Nina LeFleur — my former rival — to thank for that. Trust me, I'm as shocked as anyone, but it's been a nice surprise. Brainstorming ideas with someone who's in the same boat has been really helpful.

Another reason I'm feeling better about the college stuff is because I (drum roll, please . . .) went on my first college visit! Mom and I visited FIDM in LA, and it was better than I imagined, which was great, but also threw me for a little loop. I could really imagine myself there. But liking FIDM more than I expected to means I'll have an even harder decision to make when it comes to deciding where I want to go to college.

Speaking of . . . in just one week, I'll be back in New York City visiting FIT and Parsons. Dad's frequent flyer miles couldn't cover Mom's ticket *and* mine, but they did pay for one of us. And Bailey, my suitemate from my summer internship, said I could stay in the FIT dorms with her. I know I stayed in the dorms during my internship, but this will be different. I'll get to see what it's like to actually *live* on campus during the school year. I'm also planning to stop by the Stefan Meyers headquarters while I'm in town and see Laura, my former supervisor. Jake McKay, my friend/crush, and I are trying to make plans to connect too. It should be a great time!

The only thing *not* so great lately is how my best friend Alex has been acting. She was in a great mood when I told her how much I loved FIDM. I know she's rooting for me to go there because it's close to UCLA, which is where she wants to go to school. But she also said she just wants me to be happy. I believe her, but every time I bring up my upcoming New York tours, she acts distant and snippy. The fact that I've been spending more time with Nina working on college applications hasn't been helping. Alex is *not* a Nina fan. But Alex also knows she's my BFF — nothing is going to change that — so I'm hoping we can get past this sooner rather than later.

Xoxo — Chloe

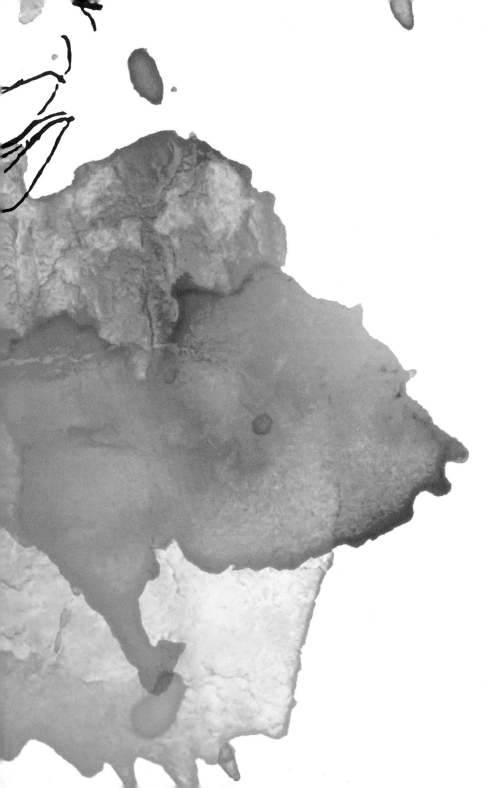

"Tell me why we're doing this again," Nina says on Monday after school as she spreads her designs out across her bedroom floor.

I let out a little laugh as I organize my own designs and place them in piles beside Nina's. She and I have a version of this conversation almost every time we get together — which is *a lot* lately. Sometimes I'm the one asking for reminders. Other times it's Nina. It's kind of a running joke now.

"Because we want to get into awesome fashion colleges so we can be fabulous fashion designers," I remind her.

"Riiight," says Nina. "I remember now." She pauses to take in the mess surrounding us on the floor and lets out a sigh. "I just wish the path was a little easier."

I laugh. "Don't we all?"

Today, I brought my pop star designs, which are one of the requirements for FIT. I have to create a fashion line for a pop star, imagining what he or she would wear on stage, out with friends, and lounging around. I chose Lola James, one of my favorite singers. So far I think my designs are developing nicely, but the casual wear is looking a little drab. I can't quite figure out what would make them pop.

I pick three looks to show to Nina, putting my least favorite on the bottom of the pile. "What do you think?" I ask.

Nina looks at the first sketch, which features an outfit Lola would wear onstage. It's a short, silver dress covered in fringe and beading. Sequins embellish the V-neck, and black beads are placed within the silver to break up the colors.

"I like this a lot," says Nina, holding the sketch at a slight distance to get a better look. "I went to her concert once. She wore this black, sequined outfit, which was fine — very Lola James. I mean, she couldn't look bad if she tried, but *this* is way better. I can imagine it sparkling under the lights. You should send it to her."

I laugh and roll my eyes. "Yeah, right. Picture how that would go."

Nina shrugs. "You never know. Besides," she mumbles, "I'm planning to send my designs to Diana Gardo."

She kind of muffles the last part of that sentence, but I hear her anyway. "Really?" I ask. Diana Gardo is at least as big a star as Lola James. I'd be intimidated to send her any of my work.

Nina looks down and plays with her hair, avoiding eye contact. "Why not? What's the worst that can happen?"

That's the thing about Nina — she's bold. She's not scared of rejection or taking a chance, no matter what the results. My best friend Alex is like that too. I'm way more cautious, but I know it wouldn't kill me to take more risks.

"You're right," I agree. "It can't hurt."

Nina smiles and looks at my next design — Lola's going-out look. I made the dress electric blue to show Lola's confidence. The formfitting style hits just above the knees and is covered in circular and rectangular patterns that remind me of the art deco line Stefan Meyers, my former boss, showcased at Fashion Week recently. Illusion netting offsets the blue and offers a glimpse of skin.

"This one is hot!" says Nina. "Really different from your usual designs."

My face flushes. "What's that supposed to mean?" I thought Nina and I were finally becoming friends, and then she gives me a backhanded compliment.

Nina shakes her head and puts up her hands, surrender style. "That came out wrong. I didn't mean your designs

aren't normally hot. I just mean this is edgier than what you usually do." She covers her face. "Ugh. Was that rude too?"

I look at the design. I let myself be more open in that sketch rather than playing it safe. "No, it wasn't rude. You're right. This was a good requirement because it pushed me out of my comfort zone. Lola's style is louder than mine, and I'm glad I got it right."

Finally, Nina looks at my last sketch. For all the edge the first two had, the last has none. This was supposed to be an outfit Lola would wear at home or running errands, so it can't be fancy, but I still want it to be reflective of her personal style. I sketched an easy long-sleeved shirt with black-and-white stripes, black skinny jeans, and gold flats. I also sketched my model with a long fishtail braid and added a gold headband for a little extra sparkle.

"I like the gold," I say, "but I need something to make it less boring."

"This is just Lola picking up groceries or something, right? She doesn't need to be that fancy," says Nina.

"I know, but I still feel like something is missing. Like you said, Lola James probably couldn't look bad if she tried, but this outfit doesn't really have that spark. You know what I mean?"

Nina nods. "Got it. What if you made her pants red and added a black pocket to her shirt to break up the stripes?"

"That's it!" I say. "It was too monochromatic. I can add a red bag for more color, too. Thanks, Nina!"

"No problem," says Nina. "Sometimes all you need is a fresh set of eyes. I have the same problem with some of my designs. Even if the answer is something obvious, I can stare at them forever and still not see it."

"Good thing I'm here then," I say. Again, I think about how much Nina reminds me of Alex sometimes. I can think of several times when I couldn't quite figure out why an outfit wasn't working. Then, Alex would come over, rummage in my closet for a minute, and find the perfect belt or accessory that would make all the difference. Sometimes, at least in my case, a designer can be too close to an idea to see what needs to be fixed.

As if Alex knows I'm thinking about her, my phone pings just then with a text from her asking if we're still on for pizza tonight. I feel Nina watching me as I type my reply.

"You have to go?" Nina asks. She looks a little disappointed but is trying to hide it.

"Soon." I really want to ask her to come with us. The more time I spend with Nina, the more I think she and Alex would get along if they gave each other a chance. "We still have some time, though. Want me to look at your pop star designs?"

Nina starts gathering her papers like she's going to put them away. "You don't have to."

"C'mon, we're helping each other, remember? I *want* to."

"Okay," Nina says quietly. I realize it must be a new experience for her to trust me too. She looks through her sketches again for a moment and then reluctantly hands me three designs.

The first image is very rock star. Nina drew tight, silver metallic pants with studs down the side. The top is black with a plunging neckline and lattice lace-up front. The sides have lattice lace-up, too.

"Is it too out there?" Nina asks. "I really wanted to push my limits to show my range as a designer. I know a lot of my stuff is more feminine. I wanted to prove I can do more than that."

"Not at all!" I say. "This is definitely Diana's look. I like how you do edgy."

"It was hard for me, actually," says Nina. "I kept wanting to add a floral pattern, but then it wouldn't have been Diana." She pauses. "Remember when I sent Sophia over for her dress design?"

"Yep," I say. Nina and I have been helping to design dresses for our school's upcoming Winter Formal. When Sophia Gonzalez, one of our classmates, came over to discuss her dress, her design ideas were all over the place. "I was convinced it was to mess with me."

Nina grins. "Maybe a little," she says. "But it was mostly because I didn't trust myself to create what she wanted. This portfolio piece showed me how to put aside my own vision and work for the client."

I nod and flip to Nina's next drawing. It's a sketch of Diana out on the town with friends. She kept the same rock star motif, but toned it down a bit. Diana still stands out, though, in a modern purple jumpsuit and leather jacket. The jacket has studs accentuating the oversized collar.

"You got to do your purple thing here," I say, taking note of Nina's signature color. "It's a nice way of combining your style sense with hers."

"I was going to do it all in black first, but thought I'd give color a shot. I'm afraid it's a little much, though."

I take a closer look. For Lola James, it might definitely be too much, but it works for the pop star Nina chose. "The lavender softens the sketch. I like it."

Just then, my phone pings a reminder. If I'm going to meet Alex on time, I'd better get going. "Next time I want to see your last Diana sketch," I say.

"You got it," Nina agrees with a smile. This time, I can tell she believes me.

2

"I'm going to miss hanging out like this," Alex says later that week. We're in my room waiting for another classmate/client to arrive to talk about her dress for Winter Formal. With formal only a few weeks away, I only have time to take on two more dresses. Otherwise, Mimi, the owner of my favorite local boutique, won't have enough time to sew them.

"It's not like we're not going to hang out once the dresses are done. We see each other all the time." I give her hand a squeeze.

Alex chews on her lip. "Not all the time," she mutters under her breath.

I know what Alex means, but I'm a little tired of having this conversation. When we went out for pizza on Monday, I told her a little about how Nina helped me with my Lola James sketch. Alex just pursed her lips and said something about how I shouldn't be so quick to trust Nina. I know where she's coming from — Nina wasn't always trustworthy in the past — but I really feel like things are different now. When Alex makes snide comments about Nina, it makes me feel like Clueless Chloe — like I'm someone who needs babysitting because she can't figure things out for herself.

"You're right. Not all the time," I say. "There are times you hang out with Dan too."

"That's different," Alex protests. "He's my boyfriend."

I raise my eyebrows. "So, it's fine for you to hang out with Dan — without me — but it's not okay for me to hang out with Nina and do college stuff? Really, Alex?"

Alex sighs. "I don't know why it bothers me so much. It just does."

I get where Alex is coming from to a certain extent. When I first came back from New York after my internship, I felt left out seeing Alex with Dan. Not only because it was stuff she was doing without me, but also because it wasn't the *only* thing she was doing without me. She'd also made a new friend, Jada, and had grown closer to our mutual friend, Mia. And it seemed like everyone was light-years ahead with college stuff.

Now, seeing Alex with Dan doesn't make me feel like I'm missing out, and I'm better friends with Jada and Mia too. Plus, I'm feeling more on top of all the college stuff. I just wish Alex could be happy for me, not jealous that I've made a new friend too.

"You're still my best friend," I say. "Nothing's going to change that."

"I know," says Alex, but she looks relieved.

I get my sketchpad ready, happy to change the topic. "So who are we waiting for today?"

Alex checks her notes. "Rhiannon Whitman."

I frown. "I don't think I know her. Do you?"

Alex shakes her head. "The name sounds familiar, but I don't *know* her know her. She might have been in my gym class last year."

Just then there's a knock on my door, and my mom pokes her head inside. "Ladies," she says, half-bowing. She always makes a production each time we get a new client. "Rhiannon is here."

A tall, curvy girl with her hair pulled back in a tight bun enters the room. Her boot-cut jeans flatter her figure, and she's paired them with a black tunic top with embellishments around the scooped neck.

I thought I'd recognize her once I saw her, but she looks only vaguely familiar. Still, I greet her with a smile. "Hi, Rhiannon," I say.

She smiles a warm, open smile. "Hey! I'm so excited about this. My band friends aren't that into fashion, but I love *Design Diva*."

When I hear the word *band*, something clicks. "You play French horn! I remember the last concert. You were great!"

Rhiannon smiles again. "Thanks so much! I love playing, but our band outfits are not exactly fashionable if you know what I mean."

I nod. The marching band outfits are black polyester pants with red shirts. Brass buttons run vertically down the fronts of the shirts and the sides of the pants. The band members also wear matching fuzzy hats. The concert outfits fall on the other extreme. They're very simple — black bottoms and white tops. The girls usually wear a pencil skirt and white blouse.

"So what are you looking for today?" I ask.

"Well, I love metallics," says Rhiannon.

"Great! How about the style? Are you thinking floor-length or short?"

Rhiannon shows me some pictures from a magazine. "I like these, but I'd like something floor length. And I think I want something formfitting to accentuate my curves."

I get an idea in my head and do a sketch. I really enjoyed designing the princess-inspired dresses, but I like the challenge of this one. I envision a slinky, metallic wrap dress with a gathered waistband. Maybe something with a long, dramatic train. Rhiannon peeks over my shoulder as I sketch.

"What do you think?" I ask.

"The metallic fabric and the fit are definitely what I had in mind, but I'm not totallu sold on the train," Rhiannon says. "I might spend the whole night tripping over it."

I nod in understanding. The train would be perfect for the red carpet, but I can see how it might be a little much for a high school dance. It's hard to not get caught up in a design just because I like it. I have to remember to take the client's needs — and the occasion — into account as well.

I get busy shortening the train slightly, adjusting the skirt to a more manageable mermaid draped hem. Then I add a cool bow flounce at the hip to balance the silhouette.

"How's this?" I ask, moving my sketchpad closer to Rhiannon.

"That's perfect," Rhiannon gushes. "You *are* a genius, just like everyone's been saying."

Alex grins. "That's Chloe!"

"Stop it, you two." I feel my cheeks flush. "But I'm so glad you like it."

"Not like," says Rhiannon. "Love!"

I give Rhiannon Mimi's info so she can get the dress made, and the smile is still on my face after she leaves. "This has been so fun. I've felt like I've been living my dream of being a real fashion designer."

"I know! It's been a blast," says Alex, but she looks worried. "But I just realized something. We have a problem."

"What do you mean?" I ask.

"Chloe, we've been so busy planning all the other girls' dresses, we've totally forgotten about our own!"

"What?" I ask. "How is that possible?" I look through my sketchpad, hoping something will magically appear. But Alex is right. "Oh, man."

"Do you think Mimi can fit both of us in?" asks Alex, sounding a little unsure.

"I hope so," I say. "We're going to feel pretty silly if everyone else has amazing dresses, and we're wearing something off the rack. I'll call Mimi later and ask. Then I just have to design something."

Alex's eyes light up. "I just got the best idea! You know me perfectly, and I totally trust you. Can my dress design be a surprise?"

I shoot her a look. "I'm flattered, but do you really think that's a good idea? You've seen the girls who came in here. Even the ones who knew what they wanted had trouble narrowing down the design."

"That's just the thing. This will take all the back-and-forth out of it." Alex clasps her hands together in a begging position. "Please? I want to be surprised."

I have to admit, it *would* be fun to design something for Alex. And I'm already using her clothing evolution for my portfolio. This would be a great addition. "Okay," I agree, "I'll do it!"

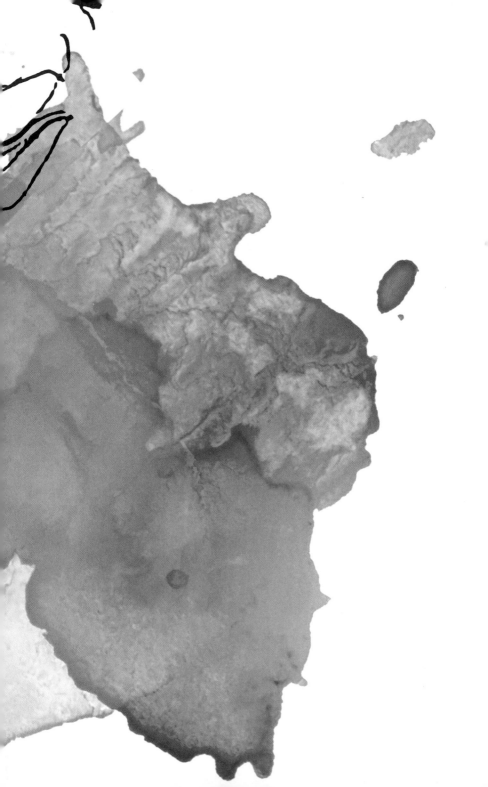

Dear Bailey,

I can't believe I'll be seeing you in exactly one week! Thanks again for letting me stay with you. Bummer that you have a big test on Tuesday, but at least it will be over by the time I get there Saturday! You're too sweet to offer to let me stay Friday and Sunday night too, but Saturday is generous enough. Don't want you getting sick of me! I'll crash with my mom at the hotel the other nights. Thanks again! See you soon!

xoxo

— Chloe

I look over my email to Bailey and hit send. Just thinking about going back to New York makes me so happy. There's just something about walking those city streets. I run downstairs to discuss more with my mom and find her sitting at the kitchen table, spiral notebook out. Beside her are five different colored markers.

"What are you doing?" I ask.

"I just want to make sure we don't forget anything," Mom replies, tapping a pink marker on the table.

"For when we leave on *Friday*? As in six days from now?" I ask. "Talk about over-planning."

But in all honesty, I'm not really surprised. Big cities tend to stress my mom out a little. As much as I felt at home in LA during our visit to FIDM, my mom did not. She stayed in New York City with me when I filmed *Teen Design Diva*, so she's a little more comfortable there, but that's not really saying much. Making lists makes her feel more in control.

I don't really have room to judge. I'm the same way! When I was thinking about colleges, I made pro/con lists. I did the same thing when I was planning my designs on *Teen Design Diva*. It's just easier for me to think when things are laid out in front of me.

I take a peek at my mom's list. She has the things she's packing in one color, the dates of our college tours in another, my visit with Laura in a third, and dinner on Friday in another color.

"Looks good," I say. "Maybe I should start thinking about what I'm bringing too." My list, though, will look nothing like Mom's. I like to spell things out in sketches.

"Your way is more fun. If I could draw more than a stick figure, I'd do the same." Mom highlights Friday's dinner in yellow and underlines the Parsons tour in pink. "Are we meeting up with Jake or Liesel at all while we're there?"

"That's the plan," I say, "but we're trying to figure out a day." I'm so excited to see both of them. Liesel McKay is a huge fashion designer — she was also my mentor when I was on *Teen Design Diva*. And Jake, her son, is my friend — maybe more. It's a little complicated since we currently live on different sides of the country.

Mom looks at her schedule. "Well, let me know what you decide. I need to color-code them."

"Of course you do," I say, resisting the urge to roll my eyes. "All your colors gave me an idea, though. Do I have time to do some sketches before dinner?"

Mom looks at the clock. "Dinner? Right. I should probably start that."

"I'll take that as a yes," I say, smiling.

I leave Mom downstairs working on her color organization and head to my room to work on my portfolio.

One set of portfolio requirements I've been a little behind on is the swimwear. The idea of doing swimsuits for a seasonal fashion line came quickly to me when I was reading the FIDM requirements, which state: *Pick a season, and create a fashion line for that time of year. You must create six to eight designs, ranging from everyday looks to eveningwear, that showcase your theme. Be creative.*

But other than choosing my first three designs, I've done nothing. My mom's color bonanza got my brain moving in that direction again.

I pull out the design I like best. It's a blue-and-neon yellow swimsuit with molded cups and seams, made of scuba material. The midsection of the swimsuit is a lighter blue, but the cups and sides are accented with darker navy blue and neon yellow. It's an adorable swimsuit — if I do say so myself! — but the next step is converting this design to eveningwear.

I start sketching, trying out different lengths and designs, and use shading to play with the textures. I'd like to keep the color scheme the same because it would make a bold statement. With my own clothing, I prefer pops of color. But bolder might be better for this assignment. I envision the bathing suit transforming into a short, body-conscious dress. I use the molded cups for the bodice. Can the dress be in a scuba-type material too? I draw the bathing

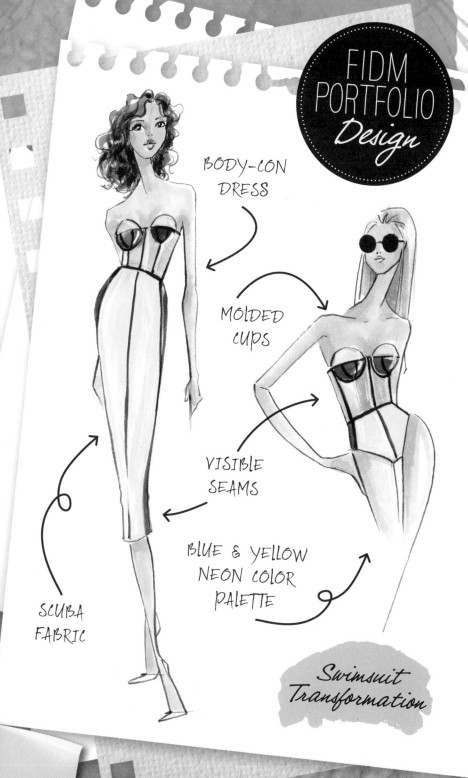

suit on one side of my sketchpad and the transformation into a dress on the other.

I'm feeling really good about the design and decide to tackle another bathing suit idea while I'm on a roll. My next idea is for a retro-inspired swimsuit. I already drew a red halter top with a sweetheart neckline and adjustable straps and paired it with red high-waist bottoms. The red is broken up by white polka dots and ruching.

Unlike the first design, I decide my transformation of this piece will be more casual — maybe something to wear out with friends instead of to a formal event. I start sketching, keeping the sweetheart neckline and halter straps intact. Then I add ruching to the form-fitting top and let the skirt flare out at the waist. The red and white polka-dot pattern gives the dress a fun, playful vibe.

I check the clock on my phone. Normally, we'd be having dinner any minute, but given my last conversation with Mom I probably have time for one more design. I flip to my last swimsuit sketch, also a retro look. I drew a white bandeau top with black and white straps and paired it with high-waist, black-and-white striped bottoms. Now I just need to figure out how to transform this design into something unique that can be worn away from the beach.

I get busy drawing bandeau tops and high-waist skirts, trying to find a way to combine both designs in a cohesive way. Something's not working, but I can't quite figure out what. I play with lengthening the skirt, and that does the trick. Next I sketch a white bandeau top and add small straps on the side to connect it to the long, form-fitting skirt. A sliver of skin is left exposed where the bandeau top and skirt meet.

"Dinner, Chloe!" Mom hollers from downstairs.

Perfect timing. I close my sketchpad, proud of myself for plowing through this requirement. A few weeks ago, I would have made excuses and decided I didn't have enough time. Today, I didn't let any doubts creep in.

SWEETHEART NECKLINE & HALTER TOP

FORMFITTING RUCHED TOP

HIGH-WAISTED BOTTOMS

POLKA DOT FLARED SKIRT

RED & WHITE COLOR PALETTE

FIDM SWIMSUIT *Designs*

Retro Casual Swim Look

4

The following Monday, Nina and I are sitting in our school's courtyard comparing designs. Instead of going to one of our houses after school, we thought we'd try a new place for inspiration.

"I figured out my casual, lounging around look for Diana Gardo," Nina announces. "Want to see?"

"Sure!" I say.

Nina thrusts her sketch at me. She's obviously excited about it. Once I see it, I completely understand why. The drawing captures Diana's personality perfectly. Nina has sketched her in distressed jeans, silver flats, and a white blazer over a loose T-shirt, then added brown sunglasses and a bright blue scarf as accents.

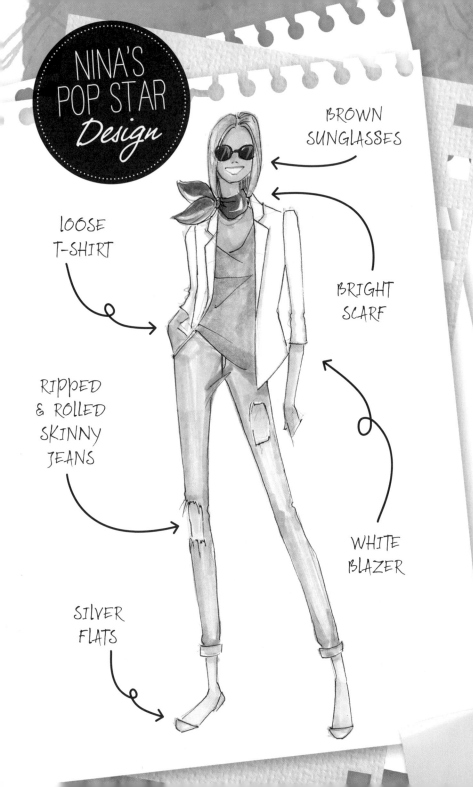

NINA'S POP STAR *Design*

BROWN SUNGLASSES

BRIGHT SCARF

LOOSE T-SHIRT

RIPPED & ROLLED SKINNY JEANS

WHITE BLAZER

SILVER FLATS

"I love this," I tell her. "It's stylish and simple, but that pop of color is very you. I know you would have liked to have more."

Nina nods. "That's what the seasonal designs are for. I chose fall fashions and went a little color crazy."

"I bet they look great," I say. "My swimsuit designs are fun, but only the first one is really daring in terms of color." I pull them out of my bag and show her.

"Very pretty," Nina says. "I love the retro theme. The blue and yellow one really stands out. What an awesome idea making a dress out of scuba material."

"Thank you," I say. "That one's my favorite."

"Do you mind taking a look at mine?" Nina asks. "I could use a fresh set of eyes."

"Of course I don't mind," I reply. I flip through her sketchbook until I find the right section. Her first design is a blue dress with long sleeves in a dark blue plaid pattern. Nina has styled it with heeled ankle booties and a funky hat.

"I love it," I say. "It's so different from your usual style."

Nina beams. "Thanks — it took a lot of self-control not to make it floral. I'm so glad you like it." She turns the page in her sketchbook to a design of a formal dress.

"This is stunning," I say. The dress is a deep purple and embroidered with a lace and flower design.

"Thank you," says Nina. "I worked hard on that one. I like how it has flowers, but they act as accents."

"Show me more," I say.

"I had trouble with this next one," says Nina, biting her nail. She holds the sketchpad tightly, not letting me see. "It's supposed to be a work outfit."

"I'm sure it's fine," I say, surprised by her reluctance. In all the years I've known her, I never would have pegged Nina as someone with confidence issues. I guess we all worry about what others think — especially when it comes to something we really care about.

Nina finally loosens her grip, and I look at the sketch. The design — a pink skirt with a cream top and beige pumps — is in the pastel shades Nina tends to prefer. It's as pretty as the others, and I really like the style, but something is a little off.

"I can tell what you're thinking," says Nina. "It's not quite right."

"There's nothing *wrong* with the design," I say. "It just needs something."

"I feel like I need to put more of my own flare into it or something," says Nina, frowning. "It's a little basic as is."

As soon as she says that, something clicks. "That's it! I can really see your personality in your other designs, but less so here, you know?"

"Hmm," says Nina. "Maybe if I added a scarf or something? What about something in a darker color like burgundy? Or an edgy pattern?"

"And a bag, too," I say. "Maybe something a little edgy in a darker color for contrast."

Nina quickly makes a sketch of the additions. "I'll keep playing with it and see what else I can change. Thanks, Chloe!"

"Any time," I say.

"This has been really helpful," she says. "Until you got here, I kept staring at it and thinking it stunk but didn't know why."

"It doesn't stink at all," I insist. "You just needed more of your unique touches."

"I see that now," says Nina. "And I'm glad we can remind each other we don't stink."

I laugh. "It wasn't that long ago that you'd go out of your way to tell me I did."

"Ugh," says Nina, making a face. "I'll never live that down, huh?"

I laugh. "Nope. One day we'll be rich and famous, and they'll tell that story on one of those celeb exposés."

"We can only hope," Nina agrees.

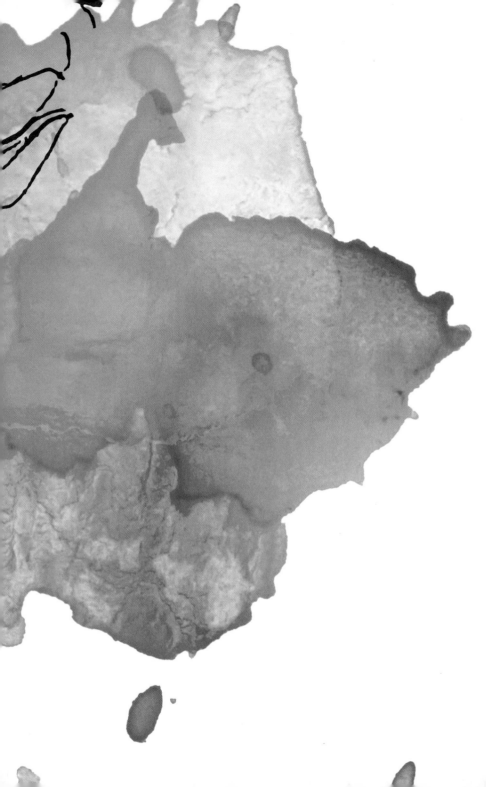

Later that week, I'm back in my room with Alex —
except this time I'm packing rather than designing.

Alex holds up a plain white T-shirt. "Are you packing
this too?"

"I guess?" I say.

Alex laughs and tosses the shirt into my suitcase. "Is there
anything you're *not* packing?"

She has a point. I'm leaving for NYC tomorrow and am
way behind on packing. I should have taken my mom's cue and
started my visual packing list sooner. Since I didn't, my new
strategy is to just throw everything I see into my suitcase.

"It's too much work," I whine. I tick off the clothes I'll
need on my fingers. "There's the airport outfit, the outfit I'll
wear to dinner tomorrow, my tour outfits —"

"Tour *outfit*," Alex corrects. "Just one. You're going to Parsons and FIT back-to-back. You won't have time to change clothes."

This *should* make things easier, but it doesn't. "Don't I need a back-up outfit? What if I wake up that morning and I'm not in a leggings mood or something?"

"Have some coffee and get in the mood?" suggests Alex. "You won't have any room left in your suitcase at the rate you're going."

I count more fingers. "The hanging out with Bailey on the weekend outfit, the meeting Laura on Monday outfit, and the going back home outfit. That's a lot of clothes!" I stop packing and take out my sketchpad. "I really should make my visual packing list. It will make things easier."

"Good plan," says Alex, holding up a cardigan and T-shirt.

"I thought you said I had to consolidate," I say.

"That was before I remembered that New York in October is probably colder than California in October. You'll want layers."

"Right," I say. I quickly sketch different combinations of sweaters, T-shirts, and blouses. "What do you think of these boots? Brown suede or black?"

"Take them both. You'll use them, and they don't take up that much room," says Alex.

"How about this?" I ask, holding up a gray sweater and pants in one hand and a flowery dress in the other.

"Definitely the sweater," says Alex.

"What about this?" I show her a possible airport look of tan knee-high boots, black leggings, an oversized sweater, and a large scarf.

Alex cocks her head to one side to assess the outfit. "You should add a black bag."

"That's a given," I say. I put the clothes in a maybe pile. I'll decide for sure once I finish my list. "Too bad you can't come with me."

"I know," Alex says, frowning. "It feels like you're never here lately."

I stop drawing. Alex has been making comments like this more and more. "That's not really true," I protest.

"Yes," says Alex, "it is." She stares down at the carpet, her face a combination of sadness and annoyance. "This summer you were in New York, two weeks ago you were in LA, and now you're going back to New York. And when you *are* here, you're working on your portfolio or hanging out with Nina."

"Actually," I say, trying to keep my voice calm, "I'm working on my portfolio *with* Nina. It's not like we go out and don't invite you. I do think of her as a friend, but when we're together all we do is work."

"Whatever," Alex mutters.

"I'd love for all of us to hang out together some day. I actually think you guys would get along," I say. "She's not all bad."

Alex throws her hands up in the air. "Now I've heard everything." She rolls her eyes.

I don't know what to say. Alex's jealousy is starting to get old. She's acting like me leaving is only hard on her. It hasn't been easy for me this year, either.

"You're not being fair, Alex," I say.

Suddenly, Alex jumps up. Her eyes are watery, like she's going to start crying. "No," she says, "you're not. Have fun in New York."

"You're leaving?" I say. "But —" My own eyes water, but before I can say anything else, Alex runs downstairs and out of my house, leaving me to finish packing alone.

* * *

The next morning, I'm still thinking about my fight with Alex. I want to text her to apologize, but I don't think I did anything wrong. Besides, she could text me too.

Just forget about it for now, I tell myself. I close my eyes and imagine New York. *That's it. Focus on New York. It will be amazing.* I put on the airport outfit I decided on (which ends up being a different one than I showed Alex) — an oversized sweater jacket, gray T-shirt, distressed jeans, and brown suede ankle boots. I pull my hair back in a ponytail and add black sunglasses to hide my sleepy eyes.

"Going incognito?" Mom asks when I get downstairs. She points at the sunglasses.

"I guess I don't need these in the house, huh?" I slip them off. "Do we have coffee?"

Mom pours us both a mug. "We don't have to leave for another hour, so no rush. Are you excited?"

"I am," I say, but I can't get my voice to cooperate.

"You don't sound it," Mom says.

I take a deep breath and tell her about my fight with Alex yesterday. "What should I do? She's my best friend. I don't want to lose her."

"Oh, honey," Mom says, getting up and giving me a hug. "That's the last thing she wants. People handle change in different ways. She's obviously upset about the fact that you might not be near each other next year."

"I am too! Why doesn't she get that?"

"When people are sad, it's sometimes hard for them to see beyond their own feelings. She'll come around." Mom strokes my hair. "I promise."

CHLOE'S TRAVEL OUTFIT *Sketches*

OVERSIZED SWEATER

STYLISH & COMFY

DRESSES?

PANTS OPTIONS

SCARVES & SWEATERS

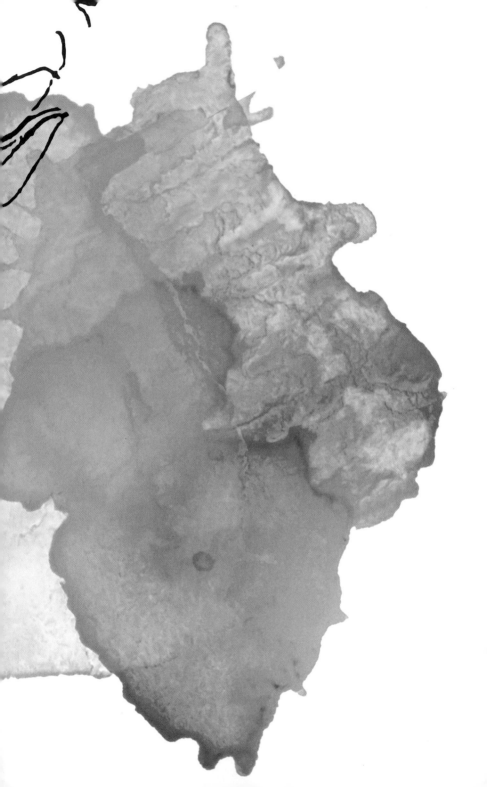

This is going to sound totally crazy, but the moment my mom and I step onto the crowded New York streets, it's as if time stops. It feels like I'm in one of those movies where the character is standing still and the lights, noise, and people zoom around in a blur. Then my mom yells for a taxi, and I'm part of the scene again.

"Doesn't get old, does it?" Mom says as we settle ourselves in the backseat of the taxi.

"What?" I ask, looking out the window.

"New York," Mom says with a smile. "It makes you so happy."

I turn to her. "It really does. After LA, I was a little scared that I wouldn't feel the same about New York. But that's not the case. It just has a different kind of energy."

I gaze out the window as we head to our hotel. I'm eager to shower, change, and get ready for a nice dinner. The only bummer is that I'm not sure when I'll see Jake. I asked him about meeting us for dinner tonight, but he wasn't sure he could get free with all his school stuff. The rest of my weekend is filled with tours and other appointments. Why is it that whenever I'm in New York, which is where Jake goes to college, it's so hard to connect with him?

"What's with the face?" Mom asks, noticing my furrowed brow.

"Jake," I say with a sigh. It's no secret that I've been trying to find time to meet up with him.

"Well," Mom says, eyes twinkling, "I'm sure it will work out."

* * *

"You look great!" Mom says as we walk to dinner later that evening. She chose an Italian place with rave online reviews.

"Thanks," I reply. I'm wearing my black suede ankle boots and a long black tunic over black skinny jeans. A white cape coat keeps me warm. I put my hands in my coat pockets and keep my head down to block out the wind.

Alex was right about it being much chillier here than in California. "The menu looked delish, and I'm starving!"

"Here we are!" Mom exclaims a few minutes later. She's been extra chipper since we left the hotel — quite a change from the stressed-out, list-making Mom of last week.

"There you are!" a familiar voice says behind us.

I turn around to see Jake and Liesel! That explains Mom's bubbly attitude. I turn back around to look at her.

"I told you it would work out," Mom says with a wink.

Liesel moves forward to give me a hug. "So great to see you, darling."

I hug her back and then turn to point a mock-accusing finger at Jake. "You!" I say. "You made me think we might not see each other." I'm excited to see him but a little annoyed I thought I might not.

"I wasn't sure if we could make it today," Jake explains, "and I didn't want to disappoint you. Then —"

"Then," my mom interrupts, "when he and Liesel were sure, only a couple days ago, I asked them not to tell you so you'd be surprised."

"I wanted to tell you. Honest," says Jake.

"He really did," my mom agrees. "I'm the one who thought the surprise would be fun. Besides, I didn't want to stress you out about planning *another* outfit."

"Fine," I say with a laugh. "You're all forgiven."

"Phew," Jake says, pretending to wipe sweat from his brow.

We're led to our table, and once we've taken our seats, Liesel turns to me. "So," she says, "I hear you have quite the big day tomorrow."

"More college tours. It's not an easy decision," I say.

"It was simpler for us," says Liesel. "I was starting my business in New York, and Jake was already living with me, so he only considered New York schools."

"But even that took time to decide," says Jake.

"What made you choose Parsons?" I ask. Jake is studying marketing there so he can help with Liesel's business.

Before Jake can answer, the waiter appears to take our order, which is fine, because it seems like Jake is thinking about his answer.

"They're both great," says Jake, "but they have different approaches."

"Approaches?"

"Like Parsons is more big picture and creative," he explains. "FIT focuses more on technical stuff, like perfect stitching, things like that. For marketing, Parsons made sense. For designing, I don't know."

"They're both terrific, though," says Liesel. "Truly, Chloe. You can't go wrong."

"We'll see how the tours go, I guess," I say. "But enough about me. Tell me about what's been going on with both of you."

Jake squeezes my hand as Liesel talks about a new fall line she's planning with Stefan. "And Mom convinced Stefan to let me do some behind-the-scenes marketing," he says when she's finished.

"Don't listen to him," says Liesel. "I didn't convince anyone of anything. Jake presented his ideas as part of a class project. They were blind presentations, so Stefan didn't know whose project was whose. He chose Jake without any input from me. Jake never even told me he was applying. So I couldn't have helped even if I'd wanted to."

"Lucky break," Jake says, blushing.

My mom looks back and forth between Jake and me, shaking her head. "No wonder you get along so well. Neither of you give yourself enough credit."

Liesel and my mom talk about getting together tomorrow while I'm at Bailey's dorm, and Jake and I have our own quiet conversation.

"I missed you," he says. "I know it wasn't that long ago that I was in California, but still. I wish you were staying longer."

"Me too," I say. "These next few days are so packed."

"But," he says, lacing his fingers with mine, "in just a couple weeks I'll be back in Santa Cruz for your Winter Formal. Save me a dance?"

"Just one?" I joke. "I was planning to save you so many."

Jake blushes. "I was hoping you'd say that." He pauses for a second, looking serious. "Promise me something."

"What?" I ask.

"Have fun tomorrow. Don't worry about which college you're going to end up at. You're in New York, you're going to see Bailey, and you get to visit two great fashion schools. There will be plenty of time to worry about making a decision later. Just give yourself a break and enjoy the tours and city."

Jake is so right. I'd like to do that, even if *not* worrying isn't exactly me. I squeeze his hand. "I'll try."

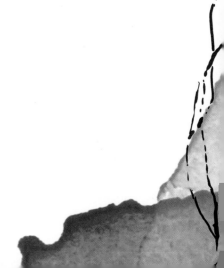

"Here we go," I say as my mom and I walk into FIT for our tour Saturday morning. I'm excited and trying to follow Jake's advice.

"You look like you fit right in," Mom says, admiring my outfit.

"I do my best," I reply. Today, I picked a black one-shoulder sweater and paired it with dark jeans and a green bag for a pop of color.

In the entry area, there's a group already waiting. A tall girl wearing an oversized black sweater layered over a gray tee, black leggings, and silver flats greets us.

"Hi everyone!" she says. "I'm Whitney, and I'll be your guide today."

"That looks like something you would wear," whispers my mom.

"That's a good sign," I whisper back.

"There are so many great things about FIT," Whitney continues, "but one of my favorites is the location. We're so close to the Garment District, which means you'll really get a feel for the city and fashion industry here. At FIT, we say, 'NYC is your campus.'"

I can't help but smile at that. There are so many amazing resources here.

Whitney looks at a piece of paper in her hand. "I see you're all interested in the School of Art and Design. Let's start there." She leads us to a large, brown building. Unlike FIDM, the walls are not brightly colored. Instead, they're plain and wooden. It's a bit of a letdown.

I follow Whitney into a classroom and notice framed pictures of student designs on the walls. That's a really nice touch. Who wouldn't be motivated by seeing other students' designs on display? It makes me think of Nina and how useful reviewing our designs together has been. All around the room, students have their own mannequins and are concentrating on measuring fabric. The professor is explaining something about precise stitching. The tips he gives are impressive, and he describes them in great detail.

"They're pretty no-nonsense here when it comes to learning," says Whitney. "I considered myself a good designer when I entered this program, but I realized I still had so much to learn. If you want to get better with your technique, this is the school for you."

I think about what I've accomplished so far and the dresses I've designed for the upcoming Winter Formal. Then I imagine myself in these seats, ready to be better.

"You'll also learn about professional patternmaking, sewing techniques, and draping, as well as how to make designs on the computer," Whitney continues.

When I was doing my internship at Stefan Meyers, I did all my designs by hand, but I noticed several designers who did them only on computer. I don't know how to do computer design, but I should.

"Let me take you to my favorite spot — the Museum at FIT," Whitney says, leading us out of the classroom. "They have fabulous exhibitions and programs. I love going there for inspiration."

When we arrive at the museum, I can see why. The current exhibition is of 1930s fashion. There's a gown in ivory tulle and gold threading that cascades to the floor. I love its glamour. My mom points out an orange swimsuit with black and gold geometric patterns.

"It's wool!" says Mom. "Seems like an odd choice for a bathing suit."

"It wouldn't be my first choice, either," I say with a laugh.

We walk around the museum, and I pay extra attention to the dresses. I compare them to my designs and think about what I might do differently. I imagine myself coming here to unwind, sketchpad in hand. I take it out now and do a quick sketch of a favorite piece. It's a gown in ivory silk organza with black lace insets. There's a teardrop opening in the back. I put a little star by it to remind myself to incorporate it into my designs.

Whitney talks more about campus life and what the school can offer. "There are pros and cons to all fashion schools," she tells us. "Not only is FIT affordable — about a third of what Parsons costs — but you'll leave college prepared for a career in fashion."

I see parents and students perk up at the mention of the tuition cost. My mom stands straighter too. I know she said we could handle a more expensive school if I got a job, but a good education at a fraction of the cost is definitely something to consider.

"We also have an annual student runway show that top designers critique," says Whitney. "And you'll have the opportunity to intern with excellent designers. You can even study in Milan for a semester."

"Milan!" I whisper to my mom, and she smiles.

"In the end," says Whitney, "you have to try and imagine where you see yourself and decide which school is the best fit for you."

That's the plan, I think to myself. One school left.

1930s Fashion Exhibit

WOOL

IVORY TULLE

GOLD THREADING

V-NECK WRAP WITH RUFFLES

ORANGE, BLACK, & GOLD GEOMETRIC PATTERN

FIT MUSEUM Designs

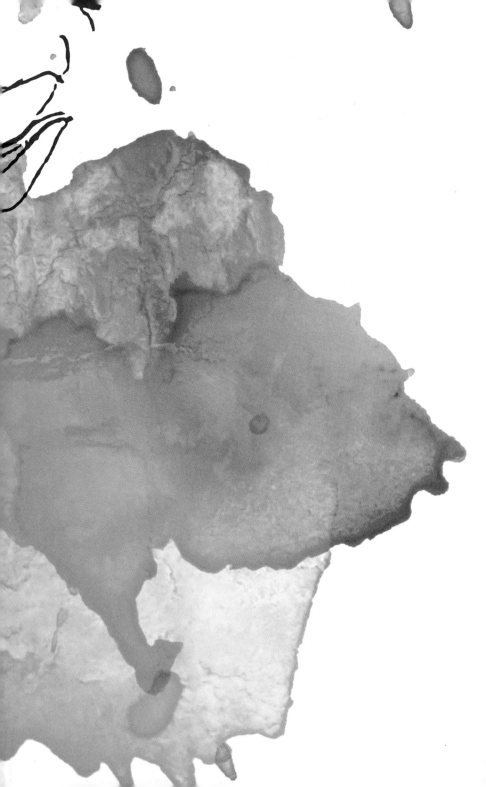

8

"Wow!" I say as our Parsons tour guide, Sammi, leads us into the hallway of the fashion campus later that afternoon. The day has been jam-packed — Mom and I hurried here straight from FIT — but I still have time to be impressed. The walls here are lined with framed illustrations of vintage clothing, all of which are beautiful.

I stare at a display labeled *Wedding Dresses* — although the designs look more like spring or summer party dresses. They're all done in white and have cinched waists, but their details set them apart. One has a ruffled lace skirt. Another has a black ribbon decorating the bodice. A third dress has a blue sash.

It's amazing how the smallest details can completely change the look of a piece. I think of my portfolio too.

From the swimsuits to the formal dresses, I've played with embellishments and details to create something unique each time. Until this moment, though, I sort of thought of my portfolio as something I was working on for the end goal — to get into college. These designs make me realize it's so much more. My portfolio is proof of how much I've learned and how far I've come as a designer.

Sammi leads us into a classroom. For once, there isn't a class going on. This allows me to really inspect the room without worrying that I'll be in someone's way.

"Our classrooms are a little sparse," Sammi says, "but having fewer distractions always helps me focus. And the windows are one of my favorite parts."

She points to the wide, tall windows that overlook 7th Avenue, and I imagine sitting and sketching by one of those or just staring out as I put the finishing touches on a design.

"The mirrors and sewing machines are another highlight." Sammi waves her arm, motioning around the space. The walls are lined with fitting mirrors — a great touch for when you're trying to see exactly how a garment looks. There are also sewing machines across the wall.

I think back to my time on *Teen Design Diva* — getting a sewing machine was a scramble, and before that we had to hand-sew our garments. I would have killed for a room like this.

As the group heads out of the classroom, a girl in a black blazer, studded T-shirt, torn jeans, and wedge sneakers speaks up. "So are all the classes in this building?" she asks.

Sammi laughs. "I wish! They're spread out across eight streets. That's something you're going to have to budget for. Always leave extra time."

"At FIT, all the classes are on one street," I say to my mom.

"Pros and cons list, right?" says my mom.

"That's a good idea," I agree. "As of now, they're not all that different."

"Do you have a museum?" the girl in the blazer asks.

"We don't," says Sammi. "But we do have our annual Fashion Benefit and Parsons Festival. The benefit highlights the work of graduating students and raises money for scholarships. Top designers who've graduated from Parsons attend it. It's really exciting!"

I remember FIT and FIDM discussing something similar. I love that each has its own opportunity to showcase designs.

"The festival has all kinds of events and exhibitions," Sammi explains. "And it showcases student work from all of Parsons's programs."

"Do you have an exhibition now?" another girl on the tour asks. She's wearing a leopard-print blazer over jeans and the ends of her hair are dyed purple.

71

"We do! Thanks for the reminder. Follow me." Sammi leads us into a room with student designs. The current theme appears to be feathers. The showcased dresses all use them in some way. A red dress stands out the most. The bodice is red satin and resembles a corset, and the skirt is asymmetrical and comprised of feathers.

The girl in the leopard-print blazer raises her hand again. "This is all very cool, and Parsons seems like a great school, but I've toured a few fashion schools already. Can't you just tell me why Parsons is the best choice?"

Sammi forces a smile. "Well, we have a great faculty. Our students leave very prepared and have real designers as mentors. Our exhibitions are great opportunities —"

"Everyone says that," the girl interrupts, rolling her eyes.

Sammi looks flustered for a moment but then says, "I love it here. My classmates are all really talented, and I love how my teachers encourage creativity. But I can't tell you what school to pick. It comes down to what's right for you."

What *is* right for me? That seems to be the million-dollar question. Too bad I don't have an answer.

ELEGANT

FIT
TOUR
Designs

SATIN
FABRIC

CORSET
BODICE

RUFFLES

ASYMMETRICAL

FEATHERED
SKIRT

· Student Designs
· Fest...

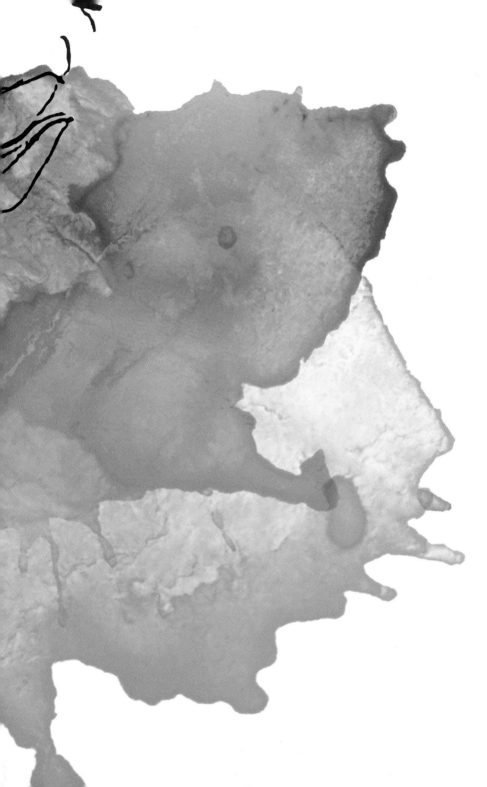

9

"Chloe!" Bailey, my former suitemate, exclaims. She grins as she holds open the door to her dorm later that evening. "You're looking as stylish as ever!"

"You too!" I say. Bailey looks adorable in a white two-piece and black floral-print shoes.

Bailey pulls me into the room and tosses her phone to a redhead in the room. "Ellen, can you take a picture of us?" Without waiting for a response, Bailey puts her hand on her hip and strikes a pose.

"So what's on the agenda for tonight?" I ask once Ellen has snapped our picture.

Ellen hands Bailey's phone back and bounces on her toes. "There's a great dance club and restaurant that just

BAILEY &
ROOMMATE
Designs

INFINITY
SCARF

CROPPED
SWEATER

BLACK SHIRT
& RED
CARDIGAN

FLORAL-
PRINT
SHOES

MINISKIRT

PEARL
BUTTONS

LEGGINGS
& LACE-UP
BOOTS

opened nearby. We've been dying to check it out because we have on good authority —"

Bailey laughs. "I'd hardly call a gossip magazine good authority."

"As I was saying," Ellen continues, face serious, "we have it on good authority that there have been several celebrity sightings there."

"Did someone say celebrity?" asks a girl standing just outside Bailey's open door. Her style — a red sweater over a black shirt with pearl buttons, black leggings, and lace-up brown boots — is very similar to my own. The white scarf wrapped around her neck brightens the ensemble.

"Hey, Andrea. Come on in! Meet Chloe."

"Oh my gosh," Andrea says, her eyes growing wide. "Chloe Montgomery? I loved you on *Teen Design Diva!*"

My face reddens. "Thanks. It's nice to meet you."

"Bailey, why didn't you tell me she'd be here today?" Andrea demands.

Bailey and Ellen exchange eye rolls. "Uh, *this* is why, Miss Fangirl," Bailey says.

Over the next few minutes, more people pop into Bailey and Ellen's room to offer quick hellos. It's so busy. Living here in the summer wasn't the same. We weren't in our room very much. And when we were, our door was closed.

"Is it always like this?" I ask.

Ellen, Andrea, and Bailey look confused. "What do you mean?" Bailey asks.

"Like people popping in, your door open, everyone being so friendly," I say.

"Oh!" says Bailey. "I'm so used to it, I don't notice anymore. But, yeah, that's the best part about living in a dorm. You're never alone — unless you want to be."

"Is it weird for you?" asks Ellen. "We can close the door."

"No!" I say. "It's actually really cool. Are the dorms at all colleges like this?" I'm sort of hoping they'll say no — then I can add this to my pro list for FIT.

"Yup!" says Andrea. "I've visited friends at Parsons and other colleges outside the city too. It's the same everywhere."

"Oh," I say, my face falling.

Bailey looks confused. "You just said it was cool."

"It *is*," I say, "but I'm trying to decide on a school, and they're all pretty similar."

Ellen gives me a knowing look. "I remember going through that. It stinks. But you'll figure it out."

Bailey checks her watch. "Let's get out of here. Chloe needs some new scenery."

* * *

The restaurant we go to is called Plush. I'm assuming it gets its name from the soft, burgundy cushions surrounding each dimly lit sitting area. "Fancy," I say when we get to our table.

"Wow," says Andrea. "Isn't that Kylie King, the lead of *Silvertown*? And, whoa. Is that Harvey Kahn? And, wait . . ." Andrea goes on to list five other celebs, eyes getting bigger and bigger with each one.

Ellen and Bailey glance around the restaurant as Andrea points everyone out. They're not as giddy as she is, but I am. I think about how excited Alex would be to be here. We still haven't talked since our fight. I texted her after we landed, and she hasn't written back.

"Ladies," a waiter says, approaching our table. "Here are your appetizers."

I dig in. "When did we order these?" I ask in between bites.

"You learn things here," says Bailey, putting an arm around me. "We called them in before we came."

"Yep," says Ellen, "stick with us and college will be a breeze."

I get a warm, happy feeling. Going to college in New York *would* be great. I'd have a built-in friend network, not to mention Jake and Liesel would be nearby. And living so close to the Fashion District and museums is what I've always wanted. But on the other hand, FIDM would be close to Alex's college and my family. Plus, the beauty of FIDM with its colorful walls, floor, and unique students is still on my brain.

"It's definitely appealing," I finally say.

"Hold up," Ellen says, looking across the room. "No way."

I follow her gaze. "Oh my god. No way," I repeat.

"That's Lola James!" Andrea practically squeals.

"I drew her!" I blurt out. "She's my portfolio inspiration!" The girls look at me, confused. "The portfolio requirements for FIT — I have to draw pop star designs," I babble. "Never mind! Just wow."

For once, I don't have my sketchpad with me. Even if I did, I doubt I'd have the guts to approach Lola, so I settle for staring. She's dressed in a black velvet top, a gold skirt with an embroidered leaf design, and black heels. I think about the designs I created for her. They're different, but I think they truly capture her style, too.

"You should tell her she inspired you," Bailey teases, pretending to push me from our table toward Lola.

"Do it!" Andrea says. "You're famous, too." Unlike Bailey, she seems serious.

"Um, I don't think so. We're in a different league of famous," I say.

"Still," Ellen says, "what can it hurt?"

I shake my head. "Sorry. That's just not me."

"It may not be you," Bailey says, looking back across the room, "but it's definitely Lola. She's walking over here."

We all look toward the empty appetizer plate on our table and try to keep cool.

"Hi," says Lola. She's even more beautiful in person. "This is going to sound incredibly dorky, but I'm a huge fan of you and *Teen Design Diva.* I'm Lola James."

I laugh nervously. "Um, I know who you are. *Everyone* knows who you are. I'm Chloe Montgomery."

Duh, Chloe, I think. Obviously she knows that — she introduced herself to *me.*

"Chloe drew designs for you," Andrea suddenly blurts out. I elbow her hard in the side.

Lola's eyebrows go up. "Really?"

"Well, um, it was for a college admission thing," I mumble.

Lola smiles. "Cool. I'd love to see them sometime. Maybe I'll wear something of yours one day."

"No," I try to explain, "they're not actually . . ." I stop talking. Lola looks like she's ready to go back to her table. "It was great meeting you."

"Same! I'll keep my eye out for your stuff," Lola says, walking away with a wave.

"She'll keep an eye out!" says Ellen.

"For your stuff!" says Bailey.

"Didn't I say you were famous?" Andrea shrieks.

I blush. I can't wait to tell Alex about my encounter. She might not be ready to talk yet, but I text her anyway. *OMG! I just ran into Lola James at a restaurant here — she said she'd want to wear my designs!*

I spend the rest of the night talking and laughing with Bailey and her friends, but I can't keep from checking my phone. But as fun as it is, I can't ignore how hurt I am by Alex's silence.

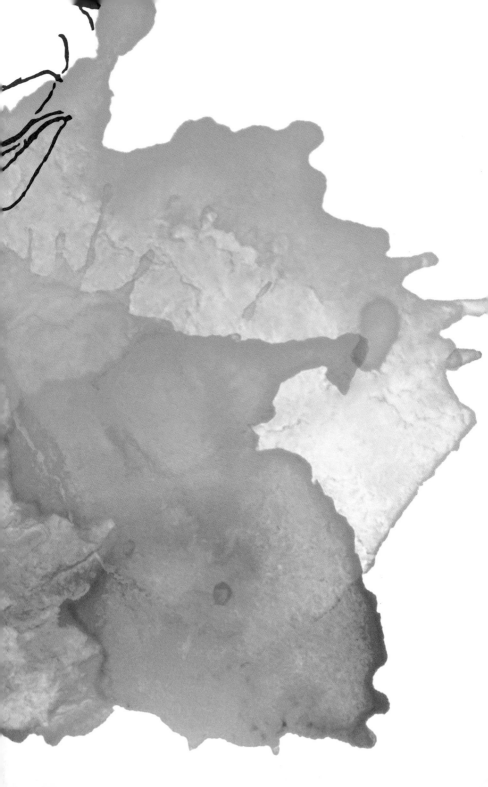

10

On Monday morning, I get a text from Laura asking if we can postpone our meeting by an hour because things are crazy busy at Stefan Meyers. I can't help but smile when I see the message. Things were always insanely busy this summer during my internship — nothing has changed apparently.

"Just remember we have to catch our flight home later this afternoon," Mom reminds me as I model another outfit in front of her hotel room mirror.

I do a twirl to view the outfit from all angles. Yep, these black leather leggings, black boots, and gray sweater over a collared shirt are definitely the winner. "I remember."

CHLOE'S NYC OUTFIT *Design*

PONYTAIL & SCARF

GRAY SWEATER

WHITE BUTTON-DOWN SHIRT

LEATHER LEGGINGS

TALL BLACK BOOTS

I'm excited to see Laura today, but I can't stop thinking about the total silence from Alex. She's supposed to be my best friend. I get that she might be upset about the possibility of me going to school in New York and maybe she feels left out, but her ignoring me is not okay. When I get home, we're going to have a heart-to-heart and work this out once and for all.

* * *

When I arrive at Stefan Meyers, Laura is waiting for me in the lobby. "Chloe!" she exclaims, hurrying over and giving me a hug. "It's so good to see you! Come on upstairs with me, and I'll show you what we've been up to."

I follow Laura to the elevator. When the doors open on her floor, I see interns and designers hard at work sketching on computers, creating vision boards, and sorting through samples.

Laura leads me to her office, which is surprisingly organized for her. "Check out these designs," she says, showing me sketches of minidresses that look like they were inspired by the 1960s. "We're thinking bright and bold."

"They're so fun!" I say, looking at a long-sleeved, above-the-knee dress with big, multicolored strokes in yellow, red, green, and orange.

1960s MINIDRESS Designs

ABOVE-THE-KNEE DRESSES

BRIGHT & BOLD

MULTICOLORED

BIG PATTERNS

"It's definitely a change from the art deco line you worked on this summer, but I love getting the chance to explore different design elements," Laura says.

"Me too!" I agree. "In fact, that's exactly what I'm trying to do with my portfolio for college applications." I pull out my portfolio, which I brought with me, and briefly tell Laura about the range I'm trying to show. I have to include everything from swimsuits to formal dresses to Alex's evolving style.

Laura gives a low whistle. "That's a lot of work," she says, flipping through my sketches, "but I'm so proud of you. I can definitely see the growth in your designs. I especially love these bathing suit transformations."

"Thank you," I say.

"That reminds me," says Laura, "Stefan wanted to meet with you, but he had a meeting. He asked me to find out about your plans for next summer. I know it's incredibly far in advance, but we were hoping you might be willing to intern again next year."

"Willing? I'm definitely willing!" Regardless of my college plans, I can spend a summer in New York. "Thank you!"

"Excellent," says Laura. "We'll discuss more this spring. In the meantime, how is your college search going?"

I sigh. "It's going. But I don't know how I'm ever going to make a decision. I've toured FIDM, FIT, and Parsons, and they all seem great. I know it sounds so dramatic, but it feels like if I choose wrong, I could totally mess up my future."

Laura pats my hand sympathetically. "I know it seems like that, and I'm not saying choosing the right college isn't important, but there are a lot of paths to the same end goal. For example, did you know I went to college for math? I thought I was going to do something with finance or numbers."

My jaw drops. "Really?"

Laura nods. "Yup. I was really good at it. I still am. But designing was always my first love. I had twenty notebooks full of sketches. I made a ton of my own clothes. I was a lot like you."

"No wonder we get along," I say with a laugh.

Laura smiles. "I didn't think I could make a career out of fashion design. I knew people did, but I thought I needed something more stable. Long story short, I got my math degree. Worked in a high-profile company for a while. Spent more time doodling dresses and shoes than I did doodling dollar signs and finally went back to school for a fashion degree. I would have liked to pursue my dream sooner, but it is what it is. At least I'm here."

"Wow," I say. "That's pretty impressive."

"And I'll tell you another secret — Taylor went to Parsons, Stefan went to FIT, and Michael went to FIDM," she says, listing off my other supervisors from my internship on her fingers.

"And they're all here," I say.

"Exactly," says Laura. "Your dream is to have your own label. I suspect that no matter where you go to school, you'll get there. You have drive. You'll do great anywhere."

I smile. Her confidence in me means so much. "Thanks."

Laura looks at the clock on her wall. "Well, kid, you have a plane to catch, and I'm up to my eyeballs in work — as always." She chuckles. "But it was so great to see you. I'll be in touch. And think about what I said, okay?"

"I will," I say, hugging her goodbye. "Great seeing you!"

As I head back to the elevator, I take a lingering look around the design room and think about how only three months ago I was in the same spot. Everything feels like it's moving so quickly lately.

Outside, I spot a girl, probably about my age, standing at the curb. She's holding a suitcase with one arm and waving for a taxi with the large, gray purse that's in her other hand. It's cloudy, but she's wearing black oversized sunglasses anyway. A loose gray sweater hangs over her fitted blue jeans.

As I watch, the girl steps to the side to avoid putting her red suede ankle boots in a puddle and adjusts the long gold chain around her neck. A taxi finally pulls up, and the girl shoves her suitcase into the trunk before settling in the backseat.

I wonder where she goes to school and if she's on her way to the airport to visit her family. Like I'll be doing next year — wherever I end up.

Just then my phone buzzes with a text from my mom, and I head back to the hotel. There are still things to figure out — my portfolio, last-minute Winter Formal dresses, Alex's dress, and Alex herself. But I keep Laura's words at the forefront of my mind. In time, I'll find my path, and I'll get there.

MARGIE

Author Bio

Margaret Gurevich has wanted to be a writer since second grade and has written for many magazines, including *Girls' Life*, *SELF*, and *Ladies' Home Journal*. Her first young adult novel, *Inconvenient*, was a Sydney Taylor Notable Book for Teens, and her second novel, *Pieces of Us*, garnered positive reviews from *Kirkus*, *VOYA*, and *Publishers Weekly*, which called it "painfully believable." When not writing, Margaret enjoys hiking, cooking, reading, watching too much television, and spending time with her husband and son.

BROOKE

Illustrator Bio

Brooke Hagel is a fashion illustrator based in New York City. While studying fashion design at the Fashion Institute of Technology, she began her career as an intern, working in the wardrobe department of *Sex and the City*, the design studios of Cynthia Rowley, and the production offices of *Saturday Night Live*. After graduating, Brooke began designing and styling for Hearst Magazines, contributing to *Harper's Bazaar*, *House Beautiful*, *Seventeen*, and *Esquire*. Brooke is now a successful illustrator with clients including *Vogue*, *Teen Vogue*, *InStyle*, Dior, Brian Atwood, Hugo Boss, Barbie, Gap, and Neutrogena.